John Sam Jones comes from university study at Aberystwyth a teacher, a chaplain in hospitals a worker within the NHS on Merseyside and in North Wales. He lives with his partner in a village on the Dee estuary.

PARTHIAN BOOKS

Welsh Boys Too

John Sam Jones

PARTHIAN BOOKS

Parthian Books
53 Colum Road
Cardiff
CF10 3EF
www.parthianbooks.co.uk

First published in 2000.
Reprinted in 2001
All rights reserved.
© John Sam Jones
ISBN 1-902638-11-5

Typeset in Galliard by NW.

Printed and bound by Colourbooks, Dublin.

The publishers would like to thank the Arts Council of
Wales for support in the publication of this book.

With support from the Parthian Collective.

Cover: Welsh Boys Too by Jo Mazelis

A CIP catalogue record for this book is available from
the British Library.

To
Clare
Hannah
Mark
Richard
Sebastian
Tirion

"The more one speaks out of his or her particularity, the more chance there is that the words will dislodge others from thinking they speak universally, and thus draw everyone closer to a universal stance than any of us can obtain by ourselves. Conclusion: start with the particularities."
Robert McAfee Brown in Elie Wiesel – *Messenger to All Humanity*, University of Notre Dame Press, 1983.

Stories

‡

The Birds Don't Sing...

Vorsicht! The word was written in bold red capitals that drew my eye; in smaller black lettering the warning of extremely dangerous high voltage, *Hochspannung....* *Lebensgefahr!* was almost unreadable after fifty years of weather. The concrete post bearing this token of concern for human life was streaked with rust from the bolts that fastened the sign to it and the barbed wire it supported. I noticed the stains, the colour of iodine and dry blood, reaching down into the bouquet of carnations laid at the post's base by some earlier tourist to the site and tried to order the chaos of thoughts stumbling into each other. After staring at the intense whiteness of the carnations for a long time I decided that whoever had laid them couldn't possibly be called a tourist.

The same thought process led me to wonder what label I could give myself; yesterday, wandering through the old market place and nosing around the cathedral with my thrusting zoom lens I'd certainly been a tourist. And a few days before, scrambling along the Orla Perc mountain ridge, the Eagle's Path, with maps and a compass, the breathtaking snow-capped peaks inviting potentially fatal lapses in concentration, I'd been a hiker or a walker. But here, in this place, without the identity offered by such labels, I didn't know who I was.

We'd chosen Zakopane for two reasons: no cheap charter flight, and a friend's recommendation. Some of the boys from the Gay Outdoor Club had been there and spent a "spectacular... wonderful... brill" week walking in the Tatra Mountains. Gwyn had said that it was like having a Snowdonia the size of Wales to explore, but then, Gwyn was such a size-queen anyway and always professed to things being bigger than they were. And after that last trip to Gran Canaria, when there just hadn't been enough sick bags to go round all the lager louts on the midnight flight home, I'd vowed never to fly charter again, so a holiday package by coach seemed like a good idea.

Griff, who always read the guide books for weeks before we ever booked anything and memorised town plans, major street names and sights worth seeing, knew from the *Rough*, the *Blue* and the *Let's Go* that Zakopane had a past. Poland's well-heeled metropolitan consumptives had secured the town's reputation as a fashionable health resort in the 1870s. These were followed by artists and intellectuals from Kracáw, their bohemian colony thriving long into the dying days of the Austro-Hungarian Empire. Then came the skiers, followed by the walkers and climbers. It was the arty connection that had finally sold it to Griff, who'd come to think of himself as one of a new breed of intellectuals since he'd won the chair at an important regional eisteddfod. And I suppose I knew, too, that he'd memorised the names of the bars, saunas and cruising areas mentioned in *Spartacus* and that Griff wanted to add a Pole or ten to the list of foreign nationals he'd knelt before.

For as long as the weather had remained warm and sunny, Zakopane and its surroundings hadn't disappointed us; we'd come to walk in the mountains and we'd done six hikes in as many near perfect days. We could tick off the Rysy, the Copper and the Sunburnt Peaks, the Upper and Lower Frogs, the Ox Back and The High One; names, unpronounceable in Polish, that conjured up the myths and legends of the highlanders who'd once lived on their slopes. On the shore of Czarny Staw, the Black Lake, resting after a hard climb, I'd taken Griff roughly, almost violently, on a smooth, sun-warmed slab of granite. Swimming, afterwards, and bathing one another in the ice-cold water, our cocks shrank to a size that even Gwyn, for all his exaggerating, could only have mocked. On another afternoon, in a high Alpine meadow, deep in the folds of a tumbling sheet of yellow mountain leopard's bane, Griff held me to the ground and pushed deeply into me; in the peace that came after sex we lay in one another's arms and watched a golden eagle circle on a thermal. They'd been good days. In the evenings we'd eaten at the Watra or the Jerus, drank coffee in street cafés and only much later gone to Janina's bar to sip iced vodka and flirt with the two waiters, Leszek and Jakub. Neither had played hard to get.

The mist and rain had begun to fall into the valleys of the Tatras on the eighth day, and Zakopane winced under the burden of a swirling damp that pressed its rooftops low. I'd read for most of the day while Griff cruised the park and cottaged in the public toilet by the bus station. In the late afternoon we'd met for coffee and sticky pastries in the hotel lounge. Griff's bit of rough in the bushes had left him feeling chilled, however, and he soon left to loll in a hot bath. I stayed in the lounge to eat just one more sticky pastry and wonder what we might do for the remaining days if the weather didn't improve. Licking my fingers clean of the syrup from the pastry my eye was caught by the questioning gaze of a striking older woman whom I took, from the elegance of her dress, to be German. As she walked towards me, I realised that all the tables in the lounge were occupied by groups of hotel guests, their plans frustrated by the weather, sharing anecdotes. The regal architecture of Kraków... the excitement and sheer terror of the raft ride through the Dunajec Gorge... the rickety local buses.... When she asked if she might join me at my table her American accent, though surprising my earlier assumption, made me relax.

Over a small pot of coffee that the waiter had brought us, I discovered that Marlene taught German literature at the University of California in Berkeley, that her husband never came on any of her trips to Europe, and that she was in Poland to visit her sister. I felt easy with her. She was interesting, liked to talk and didn't ask too many questions. She was German, but had left for America in 1947; she had three grown up sons, all lawyers like their father, and her mother, at ninety-three, still lived in a resplendent Victorian in San Francisco's Pacific Heights. She ordered aperitifs for us both and continued her story.

They'd had a difficult war, according to family legend, but since she'd been born in 1932, her memories were mostly those of a happy schoolgirl. She recalled that her mother's American citizenship had created some problems and that they'd had to go to the police station almost every day to register. She remembered, too, that her father, a theology professor, had brushed with the Gestapo because of his professional relationship with Dietrich Bonhoeffer. Then there had been the business with her little sister, Hannelore. Some of the California sunshine went out of her face when she explained that they took all children with Down's Syndrome to a state hospital, though they had managed to hide her right up until 1943.

I had begun to feel uncomfortable as the bleakness of the memories hardened Marlene's face. I sensed that her immediate thoughts, worlds away from the words she'd spoken, might bring us to the edge of an intimacy that would be improper after so little time. I told her that we, Griff and I were in Zakopane to walk, and as I said it, realised that she'd become embarrassed by my unease.

Marlene eventually breached the silence. She asked whether Griff was a special friend. I knew that she knew. When she began to talk about her son Matt and his lover Kip, I realised that what Griff called "gay man's mother's intuition" had seen through me. Eased by the new understanding between us she had become animated once again. She explained how she'd tried to persuade Matt and Kip to make the trip to Europe with her, but

Kip had balked at the idea, as had Matt who didn't consider those tens of thousands with pink triangles as his brothers. I heard myself say that I'd go with her. For hours afterwards I tried to convince myself that I was only going because of the rain.

We moved away from the blood stained concrete post with its bouquet of carnations. We walked on in the silence that had closed over us as we'd stood before the huge mound of women's hair; a silence that numbed as we looked into the eyes of a child with Down's, sitting on the infamous doctor's knee, smiling from a photograph. It was an external silence only; inside me was a screaming bedlam. At the railway tracks, overgrown with wild grasses and purple-headed thistles, we sat on one of the iron rails. Overwhelmed by the malignity of the scene, I recalled the frightened eyes and the hate-scarred faces of the people in my own village. I'd been interviewed for a television programme about the age of consent for gay men. I heard again their insults and their jibes. I smelled the dog shit that someone had put through our letterbox and the paint of the words *Queers Out* daubed on our garage doors. As my thoughts became too painful I turned away.

"The birds sing beautifully here," I offered after a while. Marlene, her face haunted, looked into my eyes.

"No," she corrected, "They say Kaddish and recite Psalms, but they do not sing. The birds don't sing in Auschwitz."

Sharks on the Bedroom Floor

Rhodri

The first you knew of the pirates' ambush was the blow to your head. In the disorientation that followed, and to the sound of excited screeches and a gutsy "Com'on mi hearties" from the children, you worried whether Justin had put his pyjama bottoms back on after you'd made love. Your unease became palpable on realising that they might discover your own morning stand bulging in your boxer shorts if they got under the duvet. Sensational headlines from tabloid newspapers jarred your mind. And where had the knotted condom ended up after you'd fallen asleep in Justin's embrace?

Penri, his left eye covered by a make-shift eye patch, jarred his knee unknowingly against your erection, pushing onto your aching bladder as he raised the pillow and struck again, hitting you hard across your bare chest. Tirion, by far the more placid of the two but looking fierce brandishing a loofah, bounced into the air before launching herself with a near primal scream across Justin, who caught her before she fell from the deck of the imaginary ship into the sea of sharks on the bedroom floor.

You lifted your nephew an arm's length into the blue sky above the besieged schooner, dropped him gently into Justin's arms beside his sister, and avoiding the sharks that snapped at bare feet and indecent exposure, escaped to the bathroom.

Justin

You had always seemed more at ease with Tirion and Penri, probably because you never felt the need to second-guess the multiplicity of motives, ignoble or otherwise, behind your actions like Rhodri did. You pacified the marauding pirates by agreeing to read more of *Prince Caspian* and the children's adventures (two of whom just happened to be called Tirion and Penri) in Narnia. They liked it when their uncle Justin read to them in English. Sometimes they stopped you to ask the meanings of words and you would realise again that they spoke only Welsh with their parents in a home where the use of English was not encouraged. You remembered the heated argument with Gwydion, their father, who'd maintained that because English was so dominant anyway, discouraging its use in their home wouldn't disadvantage the children. You, whom Rhodri considered as English as Colman's Mustard but retaining ancestral vestiges of taste for Caribbean spices that were much less bland, had suggested that Gwydion's politics might have skewed his acute intelligence. Loving you for the stability brought to Rhodri's life, Gwydion had reacted with uncharacteristic tolerance, thinking deeply about what you'd said. But then he hadn't changed his mind. After that family storm, your reading to the children, whenever they came to stay, had become a mission. As well as all of Lewis' Narnia tales you read them Roald Dahl and even poems by Larkin and Robert Graves. How many times had they shouted "Again uncle Justin.... Again" after the final "I was coming to that" in *Welsh Incident*?

Rhodri

When you came back into the bedroom you found the stricken schooner re-imagined; Justin the Dwarf was propped up against the pillows, a child nuzzling under each arm, and they were rowing in a boat, eastward around the tip of a magical island. Tirion brought her index finger up to her mouth sharply with a "Shhh!" and explained to you in overflowing, excited Welsh, that they'd reached a good bit. Justin, with a wink and a smile, carried on reading in a suitably dwarfish voice, "Beards and bedsteads! So there really is a castle, after all?" You pulled on your jeans and wondered how different the scene might be if the children weren't just borrowed; if they were yours and Justin's, how quickly would they tire of being read to and become the *diawliaid bach*, the little devils their mother claimed them to be?

Before you'd finished laying the table for breakfast, you heard Penri's crying, quickly followed by an avalanche on the back stairs. When he burst into the kitchen you took in the disaster that had befallen the little chap: so bound had he been by the magic of Narnia, he'd peed himself. Taking him up into your arms, you told him that it didn't matter and that life was hard when you were five and a half. Consoling Penri wasn't made any easier once Tirion arrived in the kitchen. She was grumpy. Justin the Dwarf had stopped reading and had begun to strip the bed of the wet sheet and mattress cover. Tirion teased and baited her little brother and said that she'd be sure to tell Mam about him wetting uncle Rhodri and uncle Justin's bed.

Tirion

Carelessly pushing a spoon around your cereal bowl, trying to fish out the last pearls of soggy puffed wheat, you explained why Quaker's were nicer than Tesco's own brand.

"Sugar Puffs are just too sweet and not at all healthy," you'd just announced with authority, prompting Justin to ask if you'd done a degree in breakfast cereals. Laughing at his suggestion, you added, rather too seriously for a nine-year-old, that you'd like to study history at university because you liked learning about the Celts and slates and you liked reading *Y Mabinogion*. And when you grew up you were going to teach at a university just like your mother. But you didn't know what physics was yet, except that it was science and that your mother was the only one of her kind.

"What do you know about slates, then?" Rhodri asked, laughing. You talked about your class project on the Penrhyn Quarry at Bethesda where some people your mother called *ein cyndeidiau* had slaved.

"The biggest slates are over 700 millimetres long – they're called 'queens'," you explained, stretching out your arms. You described with precision how the great slabs of slate were docked, split and dressed.

"I can't remember exactly how they came out of the mountain – they were exploded."

Justin asked if you'd learnt about John Pennant and his son Richard, the men who'd first opened up the quarry in the 1780s? Shaking your head you looked blank while Penri shrieked with delight as one of the nameless barn cats caught one of the starlings that had settled on the lawn to feed.

Justin

After the committal of the dead starling in a coffin that had been shaped from an empty Quaker Puffed Wheat carton, you drove off with Tirion to the nursery to look for Spiked Speedwells, Anchusas, Blue African Lilies and anything else blue for the new border. Your vision for the six and a half acres of hill-side that rolled gently down to the river Clwyd included a succession of small gardens each planted up in one colour and linked by arbours of clematis, honeysuckle and climbing roses; *Compassion* was your favourite, with its pinky-apricot flowers and heady scent. Rhodri's grand plan for Hafod Ilan Hall, which you'd bought after your office syndicate scooped nearly eleven million on the lottery, was to open the place up as a stress management cum retreat centre with workshops on reflexology and aromatherapy, relaxation and massage as well as courses on time management. There would be lots of beautiful, quiet places for your hefty-fee-paying executive guests to unwind from the self-importance of their corporate worlds.

Tirion

Driving together to the nursery, you weren't sure what you wanted to ask uncle Justin, whom you knew very little about. You knew that uncle Rhodri was your daddy's brother and that he'd been your mammy's best friend when they were students in Aberystwyth. Perhaps uncle Justin had been in Aberystwyth too? It did seem to you as though he'd always been around, at least for as long as you could remember. There were pictures of him in the albums from the time when Penri had been born or perhaps a few pages before.... But he wasn't in Mammy and Daddy's wedding pictures, so perhaps he hadn't been in Aberystwyth! That he didn't speak Welsh hadn't been enough of a difference to arouse curiosity; after all, Mrs Gittins, the lady who cleaned the house didn't speak Welsh and neither did your best friend's father. For that matter, lots of the people your mother worked with at the university, who sometimes came to the house, couldn't speak Welsh. You couldn't remember when the shiny blackness of his skin had become tangible as the difference that had kindled your fascination in him. Perhaps it had been after seeing something on the television about Tutsis and Hutus in Rwanda; you remembered how you'd liked the sound of those names, voicing them over and over and asking your mother if uncle Justin was from there. She'd laughed and said that he was from Liverpool, where you'd been once, to the theatre to see *Joseph*.

Rhodri

Watching his sister and uncle Justin driving away after the starling's funeral, Penri threw a tantrum, jealous that Tirion was getting the greater share of Justin's attention. Quietly regretting that you hadn't taken Tirion for the morning, you tried reading to him from *Prince Caspian*, but still he cried. You sang one of the nonsense action songs you'd learnt at the *Urdd* summer camp at Llangranog more than twenty years before (with thigh slapping, hand shaking and head tapping), but that made Penri screech even louder. You tried to lift him, to offer him reassurance, but he hammered his clenched fists against your chest. You thought about giving him a good slap across the back of his legs to give him something to cry about; that had been your own mother's way and it had always seemed to have the desired effect. But you knew well enough that Gwydion and Eleri had never hit their children; their discipline was based on "time-out" and loss of privileges. As sternly as you could, you sent Penri into the back living room and told him to stay there until he was ready to be sociable. To your great surprise the tactic worked; in less than ten minutes Penri came into the kitchen, his face bright and smiling (but still a bit red around the eyes) asking, "Can we let the chickens out and collect the eggs from the hen house?"

Tirion

No.... Uncle Justin hadn't been in Aberystwyth.... He knew uncle Rhodri from work.... Yes, they'd both worked in the same office at the hospital for a while until he'd moved to the personnel department.... That's right, before they'd stopped working and gone to live in Hafod Ilan.

"Have I got a mammy? Yes, she still lives in Liverpool with my father."

You laughed because he'd given you the wrong answer.

"No, I mean like my daddy's got my mammy."

Perhaps sensing that you were working something out or to give himself a moment to think, Justin asked you if you knew the name for the relationship between your mother and father. Thoughtfully, you spoke some terms in Welsh and after a few moments' word searching in your English vocabulary said, "They're married and they're husband and wife." You caught on to his word game.

"Have you got a wife, then?" you asked.

"You know I haven't got a wife, Tirion.... I've got uncle Rhodri."

You went quiet for some minutes and then asked perplexedly what their relationship was called, "You can't both be husbands, can you?"

Justin

You smiled at her logical conclusion and thought about the terms you and Rhodri used to describe your life together; friends, partners, lovers, even spouses, but you heard yourself saying, "It's called living together, we're special friends." The answer seemed to satisfy her because she looked out of the window for a long while before she asked you about Richard Pennant and the slate quarry.

"Do you know where Jamaica is?"

She laughed, thinking you were being silly, and asked, "What has an island somewhere far away got to do with Richard Pennant and my school project?" You had pulled into the nursery, so you said you'd tell her the story later.

Penri

After marking the date carefully on each of the newly laid eggs with a date stamp (that uncle Rhodri had shown you how to roll gently over the shells so as not to break them), together you put eighteen into three egg boxes, laying four under the pottery hen that nested on the work-top next to the kettle. You took the boxes to the village shop where Mrs Jones gave you both a welcome. "We always have customers for Hafod Ilan eggs," she smiled a yellow, bad toothed smile and offered you a *Kit-Kat*. "What else are you going to do to be a good boy for your uncle?"

"We're going to plant potatoes," you told her, "but we have to go up to the riding school first to get some manure." She laughed, showing the black teeth at the back of her gnarled mouth, and said, "And they're sure to be good potatoes if you grow them in horse muck."

Holding the bag open for your uncle Rhodri to fork in the manure, you asked if all mammies and daddies picked one another the way you'd seen them do on the television. Rhodri, completely at a loss to know what you were talking about, asked you what you'd seen. You described the way a girl had asked three boys some questions and then picked the one she wanted to marry. Rhodri explained that going on television shows like that was just a bit of fun and that the boys and girls weren't really looking for someone to marry.... But you lost all interest in your uncle Rhodri's explanations when one of your wellingtons got caught in a sludgy part of the manure heap; it sank even deeper as you tried to wriggle it free and before Rhodri had a chance to grab you, you'd fallen face down into the steaming horse shit. Rhodri laughed, until he realised that you were beside yourself, spitting straw and dirt from your mouth. At first you bawled from the fright and shock of it all and then you whimpered until long after getting back to Hafod Ilan.

Tirion

You didn't understand how people could be bought and sold or how one person could actually own another one. Justin's account was full of facts – like school, but he brought the story to life, just like he had when he'd read from *Prince Caspian* to you that morning. He described how the ships from Liverpool carried to West Africa fine materials manufactured by the cloth and wool merchants in Yorkshire and Lancashire, china from the Potteries and guns made in Birmingham.

"The white people traded these goods for slaves. Black people, just like me, my great great great great grandparents and uncles and aunties and cousins. They were hoarded into the holds of Liverpool ships with hardly enough food and water, chained with leg irons, and taken to Jamaica."

Shocked by what he was saying you'd asked, almost disbelieving him, "Why would they want to take your family there?"

"To trade them for sugar from the big plantations," he'd said. "One of the biggest and richest was the Clarendon. Thomas Pennant was the owner, the same man who owned the Penrhyn Quarry. My family slaved for five generations to make him, and those that came after him, rich beyond imagination from the sugar, and with part of his fortune he developed the slate quarries around Bethesda." Your interest in slates was sullied by what you'd heard, and your liking for history was affronted by what your teacher had left untold, but carrying the plants in from the back of the Land Rover you couldn't stop thinking how much more exciting your uncle Justin had become.

Rhodri

Penri had set the table for lunch and the knives and forks were mislaid. Tirion took it upon herself to re-set them and he started to cry again, leaving you wondering how Eleri and Gwydion coped with such a snivelling child (and thinking, too, that a good slap across the back of his legs would indeed do him some good). Justin calmed him in minutes by making an aeroplane from the credit card bill that had arrived earlier and been propped against the pepper mill. Penri threw the paper dart around the kitchen a few times until it came to a soggy end, crash-landing in the washing-up bowl. Your glare suggested something like "that was really effing stupid" to Justin, who gingerly unfolded the sodden bill and set it on the shelf above the ancient anthracite range to dry. Penri's attention turned to the jar of Branston Pickle, his favourite, and they ate bread, cheese and pickles in relative calm.

Tirion

Despite a sheet of nimbus unfolding and spreading itself out over the sea beyond Rhyl, you and Rhodri took a spade and a fork from one of the outhouses Justin had decided could serve as a temporary garden shed, and Rhodri set about digging the furrows for the Maris Pipers. Struggling with the fork (that was at least as tall as you) you followed on behind him, slopping sometimes over-generous amounts of horse muck into the furrows. It was a smelly job and you soon wished you'd gone with Penri and uncle Justin to plant the African Lilies and Speedwells, which you were sure weren't grown in stinking horse manure because they had such lovely flowers. Rhodri, sensing your disaffection with potato planting, asked you about the poems and songs you were learning for the *Urdd* eisteddfod, and about times tables. Though irked by his questions, you recited one of the poems but then refused to say your tables because you always got stuck after the sevens.... And all the time you were thinking about Jamaica and slaves and how it was that your uncle Justin could still be friends with uncle Rhodri after what Thomas Pennant had done to black people from Africa. Then the rain came in heavily off the sea and you were saved from forking manure with your boring uncle Rhodri.

Rhodri

Penri had flour in his hair and on the floor, and sticky dough up around his elbows, on cupboard doorknobs and all over the chair on which he stood. Soaked through by the cloudburst, you warmed yourself in front of the range and wondered where Justin had left his common sense; making scones for tea was hardly a practical way to occupy the kids for an hour. Tirion, who'd changed quickly into dry clothes so that she could join in the fun, rolled out pieces of the soggy mix for Penri and Justin to stab with the shaped cutters. She proved as menacing with the rolling pin as she'd been with the loofah and Justin bore floury weals on his arms and cheeks where she'd struck him in her play. You felt the comforting heat of the oven penetrate the dampness of your jeans and shirt, and through the warming of your body you sensed the awakening of sexual arousal. And the collision of two thoughts: the primitive and savage sexuality of Justin's flour-streaked features excited you as much as you were appalled and offended by the latent racism from which the fantasy arose.

Drying yourself off after a hot shower you heard the phone ring. Justin called from the kitchen for you to get it on the bedroom phone as he was still covered in flour. Eleri sounded a bit down; the paper she'd delivered at the conference in Gregynog had gone well enough, but she'd been disappointed by the other contributors and decided to leave that evening so she could spend Sunday with the children. With Gwydion still in the States, you suggested she might have supper with you and stay over until the morning, otherwise it would be late by the time she and the kids got back to Anglesey and an empty house. You could crack open a few bottles of wine and put the world right until the early hours like you'd done so many times in Aber. She said she'd see.

Justin

The scones weren't too hard. You ate them with the bramble jelly you'd made at the end of the last summer. The blackberries had been picked with the children along the overgrown hedgerows through which the lane up to Hafod Ilan rambled. Rhodri suggested that perhaps, if there was a next time (for in the good half hour it had taken to clean up the mess you'd come to rue your folly), you might add a bit more lard and a bit less milk. Tirion and Penri, their mouths full of bramble jelly and scone, were oblivious to their uncle Rhodri's jibe. Cut by the sharpness of Rhodri's intonation and frustrated by his jealousy of the relationship you had with the children, you felt your anger rise and with a stabbing stare at Rhodri, left them to their tea.

Much as you'd expected, you found the spade and garden fork that Rhodri and Tirion had used, still covered with mud and manure, dropped carelessly on the floor of the outhouse. You set about cleaning them, having long become resigned to finishing jobs which Rhodri left unfinished. You'd recognised the spoilt child in Rhodri in the first days of your coming together, and disliked the brat.... But those days had passed quickly into weeks of frantic pleasure when little else about the character and personality of a new lover seemed to matter, and for as long as you'd made Rhodri the myopic focus of your attentions, he, in return, had loved you in a way you'd never known. Almost imperceptibly, those indulgent weeks of passion had given way to the mundane reality of getting on with your everyday lives. You'd become more aware of Rhodri's spoilt child as an unwelcome intruder in the relationship, but you also began to recognise the shift from being in love with Rhodri to loving him, and in accepting his faults you found ways to cope. You finished tidying the outhouse and decided, since the rain had stopped, to walk off your anger along the riverbank.

Rhodri and Eleri were drinking red wine and preparing supper in the kitchen when you returned to the house just before six. From the almost empty bottle of Cahors and the glint in her eye you didn't have to be a detective to deduce that she'd abandoned any idea of driving on to Anglesey. Putting your jacket on the peg you saw that the children were quiet in the back living room, colouring-in with a new set of crayons and colouring books. Eleri had bought these with a guilt for being away a third weekend on the run. She'd been slow to warm to you when you'd first met, but now she kissed you affectionately and said, "Penri's too embarrassed to say sorry for his little accident this morning." You shrugged and smiled and said it was nothing. Your relationship had never been easy; unsurprisingly, since she and Rhodri had been engaged. At first you'd thought it was because she had a problem with blacks, but about a year after you and Rhodri got together the whole bizarre saga in Aberystwyth had been dredged up at a boozy family do. How Rhodri broke off their engagement when he finally came out to himself and she had married Gwydion within a year. After that little closet had been sprung open and its secrets aired, you found yourself feeling a little more sympathy for her rancour. But from then on you'd been left with the feeling that you'd won her prize and that you owed her something. Knowing all this hadn't really helped you to be at ease with her.

Rhodri
Penri liked bacon but didn't like liver or olives. Tirion didn't like olives either.... Or mushrooms.... Or bacon. You swapped bits of the casserole around the children's plates and quietly cursed Eleri for not saying something sooner because they could have had grilled chicken breasts instead. Justin asked her about the conference. She said it was awful and was about to elaborate when Penri asked her if she and his daddy had met on the television.

"What do you mean?" she asked, puzzled. Penri described the girl asking three boys some questions, but she interrupted him, asking with an edge of disbelief why you both let the children watch such rubbish.

"Eat your supper and don't to be so silly," she snapped at her son, turning again to her ongoing complaint about the conference speakers. During a lull in her soliloquy Tirion offered with great seriousness, "I'd like to find a husband on telly when I'm older." You laughed, but seeing Eleri scowl you replied, "You're too gorgeous to have to look far for boyfriends." Penri, pulling a face at his sister, said, "You're not gorgeous – and anyway, I don't want to go on the television because I'm going to live with my best friend, Aled, just like uncle Justin and uncle Rhodri." Both you and Justin wanted to acknowledge Penri, but Eleri gulped her wine, splurting, "The liver is very tender!" Then Tirion asked her mother why her teacher hadn't told her class that black slaves in Jamaica had made Thomas Pennant rich, and made Welsh children orphans because their daddies were killed digging for slates.

Justin and the children started to get caught up in yet another play scene from the unwritten Narnia chronicle, *Prince Penri and the Sea of Sharks*. Eleri, despite herself, was impressed with the way Justin handled the children – and with his imagination! – but drew the game to a close as the sound levels rose. Everyone agreed to do a turn in a little *noson lawen*. Penri, with a bit of prompting from his mother, recited a poem in Welsh about a grandfather clock while Tirion sang about two rabbits being chased across a field. You and Eleri sang the duet that had won you both first prize in the inter-college eisteddfod too many years ago to remember, and as it was a Welsh Evening, Justin read *Welsh Incident* – twice, because the children shouted "Again, uncle Justin" after the final "I was coming to that".

Eleri

After the children had been settled for the night and the supper dishes stacked in the dishwasher, you drank more wine and talked in the back living room. You quickly gave in to your tiredness. You slept fitfully, dreaming vivid dreams…. Penri was asking three boys questions, and then he walked down the aisle with Rhodri in a wedding dress, while the Harlech Silver Band played *Marchog Iesu* and the Mayor of Cricieth twisted his fingers in his chain of office. Tirion cut sugar cane on the steep terraced quarries above Bethesda, and beyond Cricieth's sea caves there was another Welsh incident: Justin the Dwarf rowed you in a boat and the sea of sharks on the bedroom floor snapped at your bare feet.

The Wonder at Seal Cave

Gethin stacked the returned books and wondered why Mr Bateman always seemed to do his marking in the middle study bay; why not the staff room, the small "prep" room at the back of the biology lab, or even one of the other bays? Quite often, when he was putting books back in the geography section, nearest the study area, they'd smile at one another. Sometimes, if there was no one else in the library, they'd talk – but only if Mr Bateman initiated the conversation. Gethin liked these talks; he liked it that Mr Bateman seemed interested in what he was reading and what films he'd seen, or what he thought about mad cows, adulterous royals, and the war in Chechnya. Sometimes they even talked about football. When Gethin turned up for his library duty he found himself hoping that he and Mr Bateman would be alone, that there would be plenty of geography books to shelve, and that they might talk.

Mr Bateman was his favourite teacher; he was most people's favourite really. He got angry sometimes and shouted a bit, but he was never sarcastic, which seemed to be the weapon most of the male staff used to intimidate their classes into some kind of order and control. And he always made biology interesting, even if there were lots of facts that had to be memorised. He was the kind of teacher most students wanted to do well for, to please. The exam results pleased everyone; there were more A grades in biology from Ysgol yr Aber than from any other school in Wales and the school's record of success in biology was always used by the Welsh Office to challenge the cynicism of those opposed to Welsh-language science education.

Mr Bateman had learned to speak Welsh; perhaps this was what Gethin liked best about him. Very few of the English people who'd settled in the area had bothered to learn the language, but he had, and Gethin was hard put to detect an ill-formed mutation or a confused gender; Mr Bateman spoke better Welsh than many native speakers and Gethin admired him for the respect he'd shown to the language and culture of his adopted home. And there was football too; Gethin thought highly of him for that! Mr Bateman had grown up in Manchester and everyone at school knew how fanatically he still supported his home team – United, not City. Gethin supported Liverpool and went to some home games with Mel Tudor, Mel-siop-baco as everyone knew him, who had a season ticket at Anfield.

Gethin carried the Welsh novels back to their shelf wondering if he dared start a conversation with Mr Bateman. He needed to talk to somebody. The school summer holidays had been such a mixed time; although he'd been confident enough of good grades, waiting for the GCSE results had found him lurching between the certainty of staying on at school to do his A-levels and the uneasy emptiness of "what if?". It was then that "the other thing" bothered him; it had been there for ages, of course, but "doing well in your exams" and "going to university like your brother and sister" had been a sufficient enough screen to hide behind. The kiss on *Brookside*, outing bishops and the debate about the age of consent had made the screen wobble a bit, but he really hadn't allowed himself to think very much that he might be, or what that might mean, until those moments of uneasy emptiness had folded over him. And now he knew that he was and he needed to talk about it.

He'd tried to talk to his sister. Gethin had stayed with Eilir in Liverpool at the beginning of July; he'd tried talking to her after seeing the film, but she'd seemed so taken up with her patients, her new boyfriend and the hassles she and her flat-mates were having with their landlord about the fungus growing on the kitchen wall. It was because she'd been so preoccupied that Gethin had spent his time in the city alone and had the chance to go to the cinema on a rainy afternoon. He'd read a review of *Beautiful Thing* in *The Guide* that came with Saturday's *Guardian,* and when he saw that it was showing at the ABC on Lime Street he'd loitered on the opposite pavement for almost an hour trying to muster up the courage to go in. It was the rain that eventually sent him through the glass doors into the garishly lit foyer of the cinema to face the spotty, many ear-ringed boy in the ticket booth who dispensed the ticket with a wry smile. Gethin had panicked, interpreting the boy's smile as "I know you're queer.... All the boys who come to see this film on their own are!" Only after taking his seat in the darkened auditorium did his panic subside.

It was a love story: Jamie and Ste, two boys his own age, falling in love with one another. There were no steamy love scenes and but for a fleeting glance at Ste's naked bottom there was no nudity, so Gethin got few clues as to what two boys might actually do together. When Jamie and Ste ran through the trees chasing one another and finally embracing and kissing, Gethin had become aroused; he'd wanted to be Jamie in the film – to be held and kissed by Ste.... He'd wanted his own mother to be as accepting as Jamie's and he'd wanted a friend like Leah to talk to.

Outside the cinema it had stopped raining so Gethin decided to walk back to Eilir's flat near Princes Park. Wandering along Princes Avenue, he came to understand that something had changed in his life and nothing would be the same again. Behind the screen that he'd erected to keep himself from thinking about "the other thing" he'd felt closed in silence – a silence which had left him anxious and uncertain, even fearful. But the screen had been pulled away by Jamie and Ste and their story had begun to give that unspeakable part of Gethin's life a shape. For the first time Gethin really understood what his father had so often preached to his congregation – "that stories give shape to lives and that without stories we cannot understand ourselves". Of course, the Reverend Llyr Jones had a certain anthology of stories in mind for giving shape to lives and Gethin knew that his father wouldn't include Jamie and Ste's story alongside those of Jacob, Jeremiah and Jesus. Llyr Jones wouldn't see the two boys' story as a "beautiful thing".

Gethin recalled that Sunday during the age of consent debate. His father, in a fiery sermon, had exhorted the congregation at Tabernacl (Methodistiaid Calfinaidd – 1881) to write to the local MP urging him to vote against lowering the age to sixteen. Gethin remembered the discussion over the roast beef after chapel, his father – with all the authority of an M.Th. and a dog-collar behind his words, saying that homosexuals were sinful, and his mother – in her calm "I'm the doctor, you can trust me" manner, saying that they were disturbed and needed psychiatric treatment.

Crossing Princes Park, Gethin sat by a reservoir of the city's debris that had once been a lake. He watched a used condom navigate its course on a stiffening breeze through the squalid waters between the half-submerged skeletons of an old bike and a supermarket trolley until it came to lie, stranded on the shore of an abandoned pram. He thought about his father and mother; how he loved them – but how he now didn't think he knew them at all. If he told them about the film – about Jamie and Ste and about what he now knew to be true of himself, would his father's love be acted out in some kind of exorcism and would his mother want the best medical care with visits to some psychologist? Gethin wondered if their love and trust in him were deep enough to challenge thirty years of belief in Calvinistic Biblical scholarship and 1960's medical science?

A doll's arm reached from the crib of slime in which it lay, grasping an empty sky; Gethin wondered if his reaching out would be as futile. Back at the flat, Eilir wanted to talk about her first AIDS patient – and about the fungus on the kitchen wall.

Mr Bateman looked up from his marking and smiled at Gethin; he smiled back and mouthed a silent greeting which Mr Bateman returned. Gethin put the dozen or so geography books back on their shelf and turned to talk to his teacher, but his head was already back in his books. With no reason to linger by the study area and insufficient courage to go up to Mr Bateman and ask if they could talk, he went to fetch the remaining pile of returns and went to the science section at the other end of the library.

For some weeks after his stay in Liverpool, Gethin had tried to prop up the screen which Jamie and Ste's story had so successfully toppled. The hikes and bike rides he and his friends had arranged made hiding from the dawning truths of his life easier, but he couldn't escape the knowledge that in all games of hide-and-seek, that which was hidden was always found. Then there had been the tense days leading up to the exam results, and those few exhilarating hours which high achievement and congratulation had brought. His course of A-level study was set, and before the trough of anti-climax swallowed him he got caught up in all the preparations for Enlli. Ever since he could remember, the whole family had spent the week of August bank holiday on the remote island. Everyone had thought that this year would be different – that Seifion, Gethin's brother, wouldn't be able to come home from America; but then Seifion had phoned to say that his newspaper needed him back in London for the first week in September, so he'd be with them after all. For a whole week, Gethin packed all the provisions they'd need on the island into boxes which were then wrapped in black bin bags to keep everything dry during the trip in the open boat across the sound. At least this year they didn't have to take all their drinking water too!

Their week on Enlli was, for different reasons, special to each member of the family. His mother liked the peace and unhurried simplicity of life without electricity and phones, cars and supermarket queues – and patients! She'd sometimes come in from a walk and say things like "Life here makes you question so much of what we think is important on the mainland..." to anyone who happened to be in ear-shot, but such things were said in ways which beckoned only the responses of her own thoughts. Ann Jones would bake bread every day and gut the fish that Seifion caught in Bae'r Nant at the north end – things which Gethin never saw his mother do at home. His father spent hours alone reading and meditating; on his first visit to the island, more than thirty years ago, Llyr had found a sheltered cove near Pen Diben, at the south end beyond the lighthouse. It was to the cove that he retreated, drawn back by the whisperings of Beuno, Dyfrig, Padarn and other long-dead saints, to be with his thoughts and God. Seifion liked to fish for bass and pollack, and in the last years, since his work had taken him to places like Sarajevo and Grozny, he seemed to use his time on Enlli to find some peace inside himself; by the end of the week he'd be lamenting his choice of career in journalism and wishing he could stay. Eilir painted and enjoyed long talks with her mother; but mostly she painted. And for Gethin the island was where wonders unfolded. He watched grey seals and built dry stone walls; he looked, late into the night, for Manx Shearwaters in the beam of a torch and watched for flocks of choughs. Over the years he'd talked with the marine biologists and the botanists, the geologists and the entomologists that stayed at the Bardsey Bird and Field Observatory and accompanied them on their field trips. For Gethin the island was a living encyclopaedia of the natural world.

On the evening before they crossed over to Enlli the whole family had lingered at the supper table. Eilir had unfolded the saga of the last days of the fungus on the kitchen wall and Seifion had told them stories about New York – the unbearable August heat, the congestion and pollution caused by too many cars, the crumbling health care system – about which he'd been doing a piece for his newspaper.... Then Eilir had talked about *her* AIDS patient; Ann had wanted to know if they were using the new combination therapy in Liverpool, the one she'd read about in the *BMJ*. Seifion told the grim details of a visit to an under-funded AIDS hospice, run by a group of nuns in Queens, where people died in their own filth. Eilir couldn't speak highly enough about the loyalty and care her AIDS patient's partner had shown and how impressed she'd been with the faithfulness of her patient's gay friends. "Homosexuals are still the highest risk group then ?" asked Ann. Both Eilir and Seifion tried to say something about how it was behaviours that were risky, and that the notion of risk shouldn't be pinned onto groups of people like a badge, but their words were lost as the talk shifted from health care to homosexuality. Llyr didn't believe that God was punishing homosexuals through this disease, but that the disease was a consequence of their sinfulness and the biggest lesson to humanity from the whole AIDS crisis was that if we chose to flout God's law some pretty catastrophic things would happen. Seifion talked about two gay friends, one from university days and the other a journalist; coming to know these two men had made Seifion re-think his position – the position he'd grown up with – Llyr's position. Seifion didn't think, any longer, that being gay was sinful. And wasn't all the work with the human genome project going to reveal that sexual orientation was genetically predisposed? If that was true, then gay people were an intended part of God's creation. Llyr had said that even if science did reveal the genetic basis of sexual orientation, that didn't make homosexual acts any less sinful; the Bible was clear that sexual intercourse between a man and a woman in marriage was what had been ordained; celibacy was the only acceptable lifestyle for homosexuals, as it was for all unmarried people.

Perhaps Gethin imagined that both his brother and sister had blushed on hearing this; he knew that he'd blushed as soon as they'd started talking about homosexuality. He'd thought that he might clear the table while they talked, to hide his anxiety and embarrassment, and yet, the things that Eilir and Seifion had said had been interesting and positive. Before falling asleep, he decided that he'd talk with Seifion in the morning when they drove together to Porth Meudwy at the tip of the Llyn.

Waiting on the pebble beach for the two rowing boats to carry everyone and everything bound for the island across the bay to the larger boat in the anchorage, Gethin considered his disappointment. Who was he most disappointed in, himself or his brother? Seifion had said it was a phase that he'd pass through; he'd even shared with Gethin that he and two other boys, when they were about thirteen, had "played" with themselves and had competitions to see who could do it quickest and shoot highest. When Gethin hadn't seemed convinced, Seifion talked about a sexual experience with a French boy during a language exchange when he was about Gethin's age; they'd shared the same room for the whole of Seifion's stay and done things in bed together; none of it had meant that he was gay. Gethin hadn't tried to explain what he knew to be true; but then – he didn't have the words to give it any shape, and alongside Seifion's experiences Gethin had nothing to share – just an intuitive knowing, without form or outline – without a voice.

Bugail Enlli rounded Pen Cristin and came into calmer water. The sound had been wilder than Gethin could remember and everyone was soaked. The two Germans left behind by the Observatory boat had sat next to him and in the first minutes of the crossing, in the relative calm of the Llyn's lee, they'd introduced themselves. Gethin, filled with the confidence of his A*, had said "Hallo! Mein Name ist Gethin Llyr"; he'd tried to explain that it would probably get rougher once they got into the channel and that it might be a good idea to wear the waterproofs that were tucked through the straps of their ruck-sacks. Bernd, the one Gethin supposed was about his own age, speaking in English that was better than Gethin's German, had said that it was his first time on such a small boat. When all the conversations had submitted to awe at the waves and silent prayers, Bernd wove his arm through Gethin's to stop himself being thrown around so much. Later, standing side by side on the uneven jetty in the Cafn, passing all the luggage from the boat along the line to the waiting tractor and trailer, Gethin and Bernd talked easily. The German boy was impressed that Gethin had been to the island every summer; he asked about its wonders. Did Gethin know about the Seal Cave? He'd read all about it; was it hard to find? Gethin said that it was, but that he'd take him there if he liked.

When Bernd came to Carreg Fawr later in the day to find

Gethin, Ann Jones, who'd been kneading the first batch of dough had tried to explain that she wasn't Mrs Llyr, but Mrs Jones – but that he could call her Ann anyway. Bernd, in his confusion, had said that in Germany it was impossible for children not to carry their parents' family name. Ann had done her best to explain that her three children were named according to an old Welsh tradition whereby sons were known as "son of" and daughters as "daughter of" – so Eilir was Eilir Ann and Gethin was Gethin Llyr. Though Gethin had gone fishing with Seifion and Ann didn't know for sure when they'd be back, Bernd stayed with her at Carreg Fawr and she told him stories about the island; he especially liked the idea that they might be stuck there for days if the weather turned bad. When Gethin and Seifion returned with three large pollack, more than enough for supper, Bernd and Gethin went to climb all 548 feet of Mynydd Enlli; from the "mountain-top" Gethin could point out interesting places and give Bernd his bearings.

The hour after all the supper things had been cleared away was quiet time. Gethin had never thought to question this, it was part of their life on Enlli; an hour in silence to listen for the wisdom of the twenty thousand saints and God. The last quarter of the quiet hour was evening prayer and they all came together in the small front room; sometimes this was silent too, and at other times someone would say whatever their day on the island moved them to say. Gethin thought about Bernd; when he'd put his arm through Gethin's, on the boat, he'd become aroused.... He'd had an erection. The memory of it, now – before God, left him filled with shame. It would be hard to live as a homosexual in a world with

God, Gethin thought, but how much harder might life be without God?

Eilir and Gethin were eating breakfast when Bernd turned up at Carreg Fawr. "Today we explore the Seal's Cave, ja?" he'd asked. "Wenn du willst", Gethin had said... If you like! They put some bread and cheese in Bernd's ruck-sack and set off to explore the east side of the mountain. Ann shouted after them that they needed to be careful on the sheer slopes above the sound; the last thing she wanted was to scramble on the scree to tend broken legs!

From high up on the north side of the mountain Gethin spotted Seifion, fishing from a shoulder of rock in Bae'r Nant way off below them. As they came over to the east side they saw a man sunbathing; he mumbled something about being careful on the narrow paths. Across Cardigan Bay, Cader Idris proved a worthy throne for its mythical giant and the blue of the sea was spotted with bright sail-cloth. When the path dropped away steeply, Bernd betrayed the first clue that the expedition was more dangerous than he'd anticipated; "You're sure this is the right way, Gethin? If we fall here then – das isses..!" Gethin reassured him and suggested that they ease themselves down the steep, scree path on their bottoms. After ten minutes they reached Seal Cave.

Bernd looked disbelievingly at Gethin.... "But this hole ... it's too small ... you're sure this is the place?" Gethin remembered that he had thought the same thing that first time with Seifion. "It's just the entrance that's small, then it opens out...." And Gethin disappeared into the blackness with "Come right behind me. You can hold on to my leg if you're frightened...." Then he felt the

German boy's hand around his ankle. Half way along the pitch black tunnel Gethin heard the wheezing and snorting of the seals echo from the underground chamber. He whispered into the darkness behind him that if they stayed as quiet as possible they wouldn't scare the seals. When they both finally pulled themselves from the tunnel onto the wide, flat rock and looked down into the cave, well-lit from a large jagged opening just below the water's surface, they saw two seals basking on the rocks just feet away and another deep in the water, an outline against the water-filtered light. They hardly dared to breathe and marvelled at the wonder of it all.

After ten, perhaps fifteen minutes, Bernd had asked, in a whisper, whether they could swim with the seals. Gethin remembered that he and Seifion had swum in the cave a few times, but that the seals were usually frightened off... "We can try..." Gethin whispered back. Bernd stood up and as he took off his clothes Gethin saw that his body was already that of a man. "Come... let's swim..." he whispered, beckoning Gethin to undress. Gethin followed him into the water. The two basking seals snorted, wriggled from their rocks and dived deeply, circling them both before making for the under-water exit to the open sea. The boys were enthralled and hugged one another, each discovering the other's excitement. They swam together... touching... exploring one another's bodies... and they kissed.... On the wide, flat rock above the water they lay in one another's arms for a long time, their bodies moving together. Bernd's sigh, when it finally erupted from somewhere deep inside him, echoed around the cave before dying away into Gethin's low moan.

During the quiet hour that evening, Llyr told them the story of Saint Beuno and the curlew; he'd watched the birds for most of the afternoon, breaking off the legs of small crabs before swallowing them. According to the legend, Beuno, in the years before coming to Enlli to die, had lost his book of sermons over-board on a stormy sea crossing; in some despair, he arrived back at his cell in Clynnog Fawr to find his sermons, pulled from the sea and carried back to him by a curlew. It was a story Gethin had heard every summer on the island, but then, of Enlli's twenty thousand saints, Beuno was his father's favourite. Gethin's mind wandered to Bernd and to Seal Cave and now, before God, he wasn't so sure that it was the "beautiful thing" it had been that afternoon.

Later, feeling heavy with a guilt that only Welsh Calvinism could bestow, Gethin left Carreg Fawr in search of some distraction. Near Ogof Hir he looked for Shearwaters. Beuno came to him.... And then there were two others, perhaps Dyfrig and Padarn, but their faces were hidden under their hoods.... And there were curlews; lots of curlews. Startled by the swiftness of their appearance, Gethin dropped his torch; the glass broke as it hit the rocks and the beam died. The blackness of the night wrapped itself around him and, through the curlew's melodic "cur-lee", Beuno whispered his wisdom. Gethin didn't want to hear words of judgement and condemnation and he hit out at the three robed figures, shouting at them to leave him alone. Their robes and whisperings folded over and under him and, quiet in their embrace, he was carried back to Seal Cave. Beuno spoke through the whisperings of the other two in a babble of Latin and Welsh, Greek and Hebrew, and though it sounded odd, Gethin understood. Beuno wept for all the men down the centuries whose lives had been tortured by self-hatred because they had loved other men. "The glory of God is the fully alive human being", he'd said, "and as it is your providence to love men, love them well, in truth and faithfulness.... Where love is true and faithful, God will dwell.... *Ubi caritas et amor, Deus ibi est....*"

The bell rang and as Gethin watched Mr Bateman pack away his books he decided that his need to talk might keep until another day. They both reached the library door together and with a broad smile, Mr Bateman asked, "What sort of week did you have on Bardsey?" Gethin replied he had a lot to tell and offered to help set up some apparatus in the lab during the lunch break. And so Gethin got to talk.

Mr Bateman listened as Gethin explained that he now realised he was gay and understood that he needed some support, but he interrupted Gethin when he started to tell him about Bernd and the Seal Cave... "I don't want to know if you've had sex with boys, Gethin; that would put me in a difficult position...." And he explained about the school's policy on sex education and the laws which guided it; "I'd be expected to inform the head if I knew that one of our pupils was having sex below the age of consent.... And the school policy doesn't really give me much guidance on how to talk with you about gay issues.... Can't you talk about this with someone else?" After a long silence Gethin said that he didn't think there was anyone else, but that he didn't want to put Mr Bateman in an awkward position either, and he left the lab feeling let down and lonely.

That evening, when the loneliness became too deep, Gethin told his parents he was gay. Ann said she'd ring one of the psychiatrists at the hospital. Llyr knew of a healing ministry on the Wirral that had some success in saving homosexuals. They both wanted the best for him. *Ubi caritas et amor, ubi caritas, Deus ibi est.*

Later that evening Kevin Bateman talked with his brother's lover, David, about what support he might offer Gethin, 'You could suggest that he phone the gay help-line in Bangor....'

Kevin Bateman then wrote Gethin a note to say that he was sorry for letting him down and he put the phone number David had given him clearly on the bottom... *Ubi caritas et amor, ubi caritas, Deus ibi est.*

But Names Will Never Hurt Me

The seagulls have already been squealing for an hour or more. You give in to your restlessness and lie, wide-awake, in the damp, tangled sheet trying to identify the different birds by their calls. The herring gulls, by far the commonest on your stretch of coast, bark their deep kyow-yow-yow while the lesser black-backed gulls' more throaty ow-ow-ow-kyoww offer the chorus in the dawn concert. There are rasping kierr-inks of sandwich terns and the fast, chattering kirrikiki of little terns. You remember the afternoons you spent with Deio-flat-fish on the quayside learning these strange bird voices. You'd been much younger then and your world hadn't seemed so complicated.

They'd started calling you names even before it had dawned on you. You wondered sometimes, if it hadn't been for the name-calling, whether you would even have thought about it. You'd known that there were people like that, in the worlds of soap operas, television personalities and big cities, but your little piece of Welsh coast seemed so untouched. Of course there were the holidaymakers and their antics, but they came and went. The first time they'd called you *bum-boy* you hadn't really understood what they'd meant; then it was *shirt-lifter*, and that one had really baffled you too. *Effing queer* was much more straightforward, even if you couldn't understand why they were calling you that. But then, as the months passed, you came to recognize in yourself what others had already seen. It was unspeakable.

By the time the name-calling had become a daily event, the name-callers had grown bored and dissatisfied by your apparent indifference to their taunts and they'd begun to push you around. In the changing rooms before and after games they flicked their towels at you. One day they even forced your head into the toilet bowl while two of the boys pissed on it and another flushed the toilet. Everyone was laughing when Mr Jones, the games teacher, came to see what all the commotion was about; he'd laughed too. You had thought many times about telling your mam, but how could someone talk about the unspeakable?

You couldn't tell when you'd actually started to believe you were a bad person; perhaps it had been during those months when none of your *friends* would let themselves be seen with you. You'd spent lots of time on your own then and all the bad names they'd called you seemed to get inside you. Was it then that you'd been with the boy in the toilet by the golf course? You don't remember the sequence of events now, but you do remember how dirty you'd felt afterwards. You can still recall the smell of the greasy haired youth's sweat, the taste of the white scum under his foreskin and the stale urine stench in the uncared for public toilet.

After that it wasn't just the bad names under the skin that made you feel bad.

There had been many boys and men after that first time. Despite all the promises you made to yourself never to do it again and the desperate prayers to have such feelings taken away, you let yourself be pulled into the game again and again. First the eyes would catch the gaze of another and linger; they were always holidaymakers, playing such games with locals would be too dangerous. After stares that seemed to loiter there would be quiet smiles and perhaps a nod of the head, then one of you would lead the way into a public toilet where you'd stand for longer than was possible if it had been just for a pee. When each was confident of the other's intention – a kind of knowing that you came to understand and which became more certain with experience – a place would be negotiated; a tent or a beach hut, even the rocks and caves at the bottom of the cliffs. Caravans were best of all because the curtains could be drawn and the door locked. Failing these options, and if you both were desperate enough, it would be in a toilet cubicle against walls smeared with lurid messages and cartoon phalluses.

Sometimes, when you let yourself remember, the shame suffocated you. At such times you tried to recall what legacy these liaisons and encounters left you to be grateful for. Sex education at Ysgol-y-Traeth, its curriculum barely discussed by the embarrassed, middle-aged, respectable chapel-goers on the governing board, had failed to acknowledge the real world of AIDS and unplanned pregnancies. It was these men and boys, in holiday shorts and suntan cream, who'd taught you about using condoms and safer sex. Some had even shown tenderness.

Others had been brutish, especially in the days of your inexperience, taking what they wanted by threat or by force.... Not that you'd ever been beaten up... you'd never had to lie about a swollen lip or a black eye. Even those who'd said *yes* to your *nos* hadn't been violent in that sense; they'd just held you down more firmly than was comfortable and pushed harder. You'd soon learned that clenching the muscle as tight as possible only made it hurt more so your *no* was usually interpreted as a *yes* because you relaxed to save yourself the pain. After learning about KY or using loads of spit, with the boy from Wolverhampton – the one you'd seen every day for a fortnight because you'd liked one another, it became easier and more convenient to say *yes* even though you never liked it. And so any possible nastiness had been avoided.

The alarm clock ringing out from your parents' bedroom breaks through the thoughts and the seagulls. Your attic bedroom, with sloping ceilings and sea view, is still stifling from the previous day's heat. The white tee-shirt you wore the night before, stained at the armpits, is lying over the back of a dining chair that looks curiously out of place next to the small chest of drawers. On the chest, amid the clutter of deodorant cans, after-shave bottles and tubes of creams for spots and athlete's foot, the two ten-pound notes are where you left them. You try again to remember a forgotten errand or any other reason why they should have been in the back left-hand pocket of your jeans. You don't want to accept that the slightly drunk American with the snake tattoo coiled around his thigh, its head questioning at his pubic hair, must be the source of such munificence. Twice you'd told him that you didn't take money and that as long as he used a condom with plenty of lube you didn't mind. He must have put the two notes into your pocket when you went to the toilet in the cramped camper van after you'd had sex. You wonder why the snake man had felt the need to pay for something you'd been willing enough to give.

As you shower that sunny August morning of your seventeenth birthday, you think about all the hurtful names you've ever been called. There'd been *effing queer*; there'd been *turd-driver* and *arse-bandit*. Rent-boy, though, didn't sound so bad.

My Velvet Eyes

Prysor Lewis lay, still and shrunken, in a tangle of tubes and wires. Staring at the bedside monitor, fascinated by the peaks and troughs, Sam could recognise none of the feelings he thought a son might have at a father's deathbed. He'd even found himself fantasising about Frank, his father's nurse, wondering if the three studs in his left ear were an indication that there may be other pierced bits under his uniform. Slouched in a chair at the dying man's side, his arms folded across his chest, he tweaked the nipple rings through the cotton of his own tee shirt unconsciously and thought about what sex with Frank might be like.

After some time, he wondered what Sawel Rhys would have felt. Maybe hurt and anger at his father's rejection? But Sam's invention of himself had so displaced Sawel that he couldn't reinvent the mindset of his former self. He remembered his father's pronouncement: "A gay son is as good as a dead son!" Obediently Sawel Rhys Lewis, that timid little Welsh son, had let himself wither away. Sam Rees, young gay man about town, had taken his place. No more Welsh novels, Welsh rock or

S4C for Sam; he was into Manchester pink politics and HIV support networks. And when Prysor had excluded him from his own mother's funeral, Sawel had allowed himself to be buried with her.

He was only at the hospital now because of his sister Jane. Adrian had tried to dissuade him from backing out of their planned walking trip, but four kids under ten, a three hundred mile journey with snow in the Borders, and a husband on a business trip abroad had made it hard to argue with her. She'd get there when she could.

When Sam had arrived at the hospital the nurse had taken him to one side and warned him gently of Prysor's grave prognosis. Despite the antibiotics they were pouring into him, the septicaemia seemed to be knocking out all his vital organ functions, one by one. He'd cautioned Sam of the peculiar contrasts of his father's state, combining periods of lucidness with confused babble and total lapses of consciousness. But it was only when the regular lines skipped out of their pattern, breaking the screen's mesmerising grip on Sam, that he realised he couldn't remain a passive observer at his father's mute death bed. The old man had returned.

Prysor Lewis, oblivious to his son's presence, began to speak. He admonished a patient for inadequate flossing and asked the nurse to mix an amalgam: for ever the dentist he'd returned to his surgery…. But then, to Sam's incredulous ears, he began to speak in Spanish.

"Rubén, Rubén," he called. "Ot-ra-vez, Rubén... ot-ra-vez... dam-ef-uego." The words were meaningless to him, apart from scattered Welsh and English references to newspapers and "the big scandal", but he jotted them down, noting in particular a phrase repeated endlessly by his father, "Mi-soch-os-de-ter-theo-pelo".

Adrian wasn't home. Sam absently scanned his note suggesting that they might meet at the gym and moved quickly on to check the answering machine. He heard Jane's voice and Prysor was dead. Through her tears Sam grasped her suggestions for meeting up with him to sort out death's practical aftermath. He dialled her number but the phone rang out; she'd put her plans into action and was on her way.

Untouched by the news of Prysor's demise, Sam remembered that he and Adrian had planned to be away for the week. He stared into the empty fridge and decided to do a shop; Adrian would have to eat if he decided not to go with them to Wales and he and Jane would need to take some stuff with them.... He realised that the decision to stay with Jane in Dolgellau, sorting out Prysor's affairs and arranging the funeral, had already been made. The ghost of Sawel Rhys had nudged his conscience too sharply for Sam to leave these matters entirely to his sister.

Adrian didn't know what to think when he saw Sam sprawled out on the living-room floor surrounded by bags of shopping and the voice of Welsh hymns washing over him. But then he saw Sam's tears and he knew well enough. Adrian lay with Sam, hugging him for a long time, kissing the back of his neck and stroking his hair. Some time later the tears ran dry.

Jane was exhausted. She introduced little Euan Crawford Sinclair to his uncles; he'd cried all the way from Carlisle! Remembering that the hospital had also referred to his sister as Crawford, Sam puzzled over this addition to their names, but as he hugged Jane and her own tears flowed again, Prysor's death took their thoughts in other directions.

Later in the evening their conversation took an enigmatic turn when Jane tentatively announced, "There's an addition to the family that I haven't told you about.... No – I'm not pregnant! But hold on to your seat or this might blow you away." The family had always believed that Jane's mother had died when she was eleven months old, Prysor later marrying Sam's mother. But Jane told a very different story: Margaret Crawford Lewis, her mother, wasn't dead. "She spent nearly twenty years in prison, convicted of the murder of her lover, Rubén Ibarruri!"

Jane explained that the Crawfords were wealthy Scottish landowners, and whilst they'd seen to it that Margaret was living comfortably, they'd also paid some clever lawyers to skip over her in the line of inheritance. About two or three years ago they'd written to tell her that she would become a very rich woman one day, the only condition being that she and her children carried the Crawford name.

"And Margaret?" Adrian asked. "Have you met her?"

"Oh yes," Jane smiled, "many times. She's lovely," she held Sam's hand across the table, "but Eluned was our mother."

"This Rubén...Spanish, was he?" Sam asked, recalling Prysor's delirium.

"Yes... from the Basque country. Don't you remember seeing photos of him in one of the old albums in Cefn Llwyd? He was a dentist, too; he studied with dad in London and they shared a bed sit."

Sam shook his head.

"Why did Margaret kill him, do you know?" Adrian asked.

Jane bit her lip and after a long sigh she got up from the table. Walking to one of her bags, which was still in the hall, she said, "I think we'd better open the bottle I brought you both; it's not an easy story to tell and it may even be a harder story to hear."

She put the Glenfiddich on the table and Sam reached for some clean glasses. But as Adrian began to pour, Euan started crying in the spare room.

While Jane was upstairs feeding the baby, Sam and Adrian cleared the table, washed the few dishes and wondered, over the Glenfiddich, why Margaret had killed her lover and what kind of wealth Jane might be coming into. When she still hadn't returned after nearly twenty minutes Sam went looking for her. She and Euan were sound asleep. A little later, before sleep overtook Sam, Adrian said to him, "I hope I'm not going to lose Sam Rees.... He's the man I fell in love with. That boy who was talking in Welsh to his sister in our kitchen earlier tonight: who was he?"

Sam held Adrian in his arms until he slept.

They got to Dolgellau late the next afternoon. Jane had been business-like and efficient dealing with the paper work at the hospital in Wrexham, which was more than could be said for the hospital staff that they dealt with. She and Sam were grateful that Euan had taken so well to Adrian; they'd gone off for a walk in the winter sunshine and discovered a beautiful old walled garden ablaze with crocus, Lenten roses and fair maids of February that Adrian assumed had probably been a part of an estate that the new, sprawling hospital had devoured. Among Prysor's few belongings, handed over to Jane at the hospital, they found a bunch of keys that they trusted would let them into Cefn Llwyd.

Turning up the drive to the old house Jane asked Sam to stop the car.

"I want to say something about Prysor's estate," she said, reaching into her bag for the bunch of keys she'd been handed in the hospital. "Here, you take these." She pushed her hand through her hair and turned in her seat so that she could also see Adrian in the back with Euan. With some hesitation she said, "All this may be a bit premature because I don't know anything about Prysor's will. I know that we're all the family he had and that he didn't have anything to do with you two, so it would seem likely that he's cut you out…"

"There's no need for this, Jane," Sam interrupted, tossing

the keys gently into her lap.

"Sam, let me finish," she said and sighed. "I don't know what we'll find in his sock drawers or under the mattresses, but whatever he's left to me, I'll get our solicitor in Edinburgh to transfer to you."

"No Jane, don't do this," Sam said, shaking his head. "He doesn't owe me anything and I've got no expectation that I'm included. I'm here to support you. Isn't that right, Ady?"

"No…" Adrian searched for words and waved his hands, "don't bring me into it. This is one of those times I'm grateful that the law doesn't recognise our marital bliss. This has got to be between the two of you."

A silence fell heavily over them. Adrian tried to lift them out of it: "You've got to admit though Sam, the house would make a lovely gay B & B. I bet we'd make a bomb with all those butch mountaineers from the Gay Outdoor Club. We could do all the exterior paint-work pink and advertise in *Gay Times*."

They all laughed and Sam drove on to the house.

Even before they'd emptied the car a neighbour turned up, a bottle of milk and a loaf of bread in her basket. Before they sat down to eat that evening four other callers had paid their respects and left them with an apple tart, a Victoria sponge, a dozen fresh eggs collected that day and a basket of winter vegetables. Adrian, who'd lived all his life in various Manchester suburbs, had never witnessed that kind of pulling-together in a community. Jane sat at the large oak table in the kitchen feeding Euan while Sam cooked. Their conversation had lapsed and Jane spoke sweet nothings to the baby at her breast.

"What was that you said to Euan?" Sam asked.

"Oh…. It's just something Margaret says to him…. I'm not even sure I pronounce it properly."

"Say it for me, Jane." It was almost a command.
She looked curiously at her brother, saying, "It's something like *Mis ojos de terciopelo*."

"What does it mean, Jane?" Sam asked sharply.

"I don't know exactly; it's something like 'my velvet eyes'. It's just one of those sweet things you say to babies… or to your boy or girlfriend. What's the matter, Sam? Tell me."

"When I sat with Prysor yesterday morning he was quite delirious and that was one of the things he kept saying."

"Oh, I see…. Well, like I said, it's one of Margaret's sayings. Perhaps it's something she used to say to him."

"Sure, that makes sense, I suppose," Sam said, turning back to the Aga which he still hadn't quite got the hang of.

It was Sam, after they'd eaten, who finally suggested that they look for Prysor's papers. Adrian volunteered to wash the dishes but Jane was anxious that they went through things together. They found his desk orderly and its contents mostly filed neatly away in clearly identified folders; buildings insurance, utilities, BT & gas shares, bank statements, credit card accounts, car…. An old wallet contained a wad of £20 notes. Jane counted the money and handed it to Sam, who gave it back to her and said they'd better look for a copy of the will so that they'd have some idea what to do with it. Adrian found some old photographs, wrapped carefully in a paper bag and held together with an elastic band. Jane looked through them and recognised Margaret in her wedding gown; another was of the wedding party.

"Wasn't Prysor handsome when he was young?" she said, pointing him out to Adrian.

"Hmm…. His brother was pretty cute too; was he the best man?" Adrian asked.

Jane looked at the man he was pointing to: "Oh…. That's Rubén Ibarruri; he was their best man. It's funny, until you mentioned it I never realised how much alike they were. Look Sam," she said, passing the photograph to him.

Adrian poured the contents of another envelope onto the hearthrug: "These are old club membership cards going back years and…. Cor…. Look at this. A blood donor book with little stamps inside it for every donation he made; he was 'AB'. What are you Sam?"

Jane made a low moan and pushed her fingers through her hair.

"Is this too much for you Jane?" Sam asked. "Would you rather leave it until tomorrow?"

"I'm 'O'," Jane said quietly. "My blood group is 'O'."

"No Jane. Not if dad was 'AB'. You can't be Group 'O'," Sam corrected her.

"I'm 'O'," she said determinedly. "Margaret knew it all along. She told me, you know, the second time I met her. I thought she was just being mischievous; that twenty years in jail

62

had made her bitter. She told me I was Rubén Ibarruri's daughter.... But honestly, I didn't want the proof of it. Prysor was my dad. But here we have it – all the proof we need."

She picked up the little book filled with stamps, and she wept. Both Sam and Adrian held her for a long time.

Much later, after they'd drunk a few glasses of Prysor's Laphroaig, Adrian said, "None of this really makes sense to me. Why did Margaret kill Rubén Ibarruri if they were lovers and she knew him to be your father?"

"He took another lover," Jane said.

"God... That's a bit over the top, isn't it?" Adrian quizzed. "I mean, killing him just because he found another woman. She was married after all.... He was only doing to her what she was doing to Prysor."

"Rubén's new lover was a man and that made Margaret angry as well as jealous."

And Sam heard Prysor calling out for Rubén: *Mis ojos de terciopelo.*

The Magenta Silk Thread

Mrs Amelia Roberts had waited on the platform for the eight eighteen to Shrewsbury for a good ten minutes before the train pulled in. The wind, which came right through the town off Cardigan Bay, carried a light drizzle, and in the fifteen minute walk to the station from Prince of Wales Crescent it had left her feeling chilled; through her Aquascutum rain coat and navy Viyella suit she felt the dampness niggle the rheumatic in her hip. She'd thought of phoning for a taxi when she'd pulled back the heavy velvet curtains of the front sitting-room bay window and seen the overcast seascape, but Cader Cabs had let her down twice before. Run by a local boy, too. It was a shame he was so unreliable; with that rough crowd from the Midlands moving in and buying up everything, she liked to support the few locals still in business, but.... While she was generous enough to give people the opportunity to make amends, no one ever got a third chance with Mrs Amelia Roberts.

It hadn't occurred to her that at seventy-seven the trip to Shrewsbury might be too much for her. She couldn't remember the last time she'd taken the train; for years now, if she'd wanted to go shopping for clothes, or even just fancied a day out to Chester or Llandudno – or that nice Cheshire Oaks place in Ellesmere Port, she'd go in the car with Megan *Paris House,* always making sure she paid for their lunch and half the petrol. But this time she'd said nothing to Megan; as well as they both knew one another, she wasn't sure what her friend would make of it all. This occasion was different.... Yes, a very different kind of event - and very special, and she didn't want anything that Megan might say to spoil it. Taking the train saved Amelia Roberts from having to explain.

She'd never liked crossing Barmouth Bridge on the train; when the tide was high and the wind blew in off the sea, the windows would be splashed by the waves and it was all too unnerving.... And since those worms had been eating away at the wooden piles she'd decided the bridge probably wasn't safe anyway, despite all the thousands of pounds British Rail had paid to repair it. As the train pulled slowly out over the swollen estuary she willed herself to think about something pleasant for the next five minutes; after that she could relax and enjoy the countryside.

It was her Jack's smiling face that came to her: fresh and freckled, his green eyes ablaze under all those foxy curls. They were dancing; one of the regular Saturday night dos in the assembly room with the local third-rate dance band playing all the songs from *Top Hat* and *Follow the Fleet* (that had just shown in the White Cinema) led by Eddie Jones; despite blackheads and dirty fingernails from shovelling in the coal yard, he sang *Cheek to Cheek* thinking he was every girl's answer to Fred Astaire. She felt Jack squeeze her to him as they moved across the dance floor; in her Jack's arms she wondered about the things that never were because of those German bullets on a beach near Boulogne. Their years of married life together. Their children growing up and having families of their own. How well Jack would have aged with those high cheekbones and how he would have enjoyed their grandchildren. None of it hurt like it used to. Was that because old age had brought her wisdom or had her heart just hardened after fifty-eight years a widow? She was just glad that it had stopped hurting. Had anyone been sitting opposite Mrs Amelia Roberts as the train crossed over the estuary bridge, they may have seen the fingers of a gloved hand dance on the arm-rest to an inaudible rhythm and perhaps glimpsed the quiet smile on a face that looked at peace with the world.

When the train pulled away from the coast in its faltering dash across Montgomeryshire towards Newtown, the late summer countryside emerged from the clinging shroud of coastal mizzle and the bright sunshine enlivened the land's fading colours. Mrs Amelia Roberts' face flushed, though no one sat close enough to notice, as she remembered that she'd left the chamber under her high brass bed with the previous night's two offerings unemptied. She wondered, if fate were to play some cruel tricks on her that day, a train disaster or a heart attack, what Betty-next-door would think when she took her spare key and began to rummage. And she laughed to herself when she thought about the other little treasures Betty might find that would make the piss pot seem incidental.

Thinking about Betty-next-door made her think about Nellie Bet, who, in turn, made her think about Glyn. It was for him she was making the effort; buying a new rig-out when she had a wardrobe full of Jaeger and Viyella. It was a shame that Nellie Bet hadn't lived to see it; she'd done nothing about that diabetes for years and in the end she'd just let herself go until the gangrene was stinking. But then, had she lived, none of it would be happening in quite the same way and she wouldn't have been sitting on the train going to Shrewsbury. Of course she'd missed Nellie Bet these past eighteen months; they'd known one another all their lives.... It was she who'd told her, after the telegram, that she had to get on with her life.

"Milli," she'd said, "war is war and your Jack's dead. You don't owe it to him to be a mourning virgin for the rest of your life." But what she'd given to her Jack she couldn't give to anyone else and despite many an overture it was as Mrs Jack Roberts she'd remained, until, hardly without noticing, Jack was forgotten by most of the town's folk as they took to calling her Mrs Amelia Roberts.

Nellie Bet never forgot. She always made sure that "Our Milli" was part of her family; matron of honour at her wedding, god mother to Lois and Griff, and always expected for Sunday dinner and Christmas Day. And then, when Glyn had come along, a real after-thought at forty-two, Nellie Bet took to leaving him for hours on end with her in the shop. The summer visitors who came to Morgan's Woollens to buy hand-knits and yarns, and skirt lengths from the mill in Trefriw, knowing no better, used to think she was his mother. Even if she did sometimes secretly think of Glyn as her own child, as Nellie Bet's gift to her, Amelia Roberts had never claimed him as her own.

Certainly she'd wiped Glyn's bottom, fed him *Ostermilk* and burped him more times than Nellie Bet had ever done. She'd read him stories and helped with his homework, and taken him on his first visit to Chester Zoo because he wanted to see real elephants. It was to her he'd come to be tutored in his recitations for all the different local eisteddfods because his Mam had said that Anti Mill had got more patience, and she'd taken him to the Dragon Theatre to see summer shows, pantomimes and Gilbert and Sullivan. Hadn't it been the comfort and reassurance she offered, not his mother's, that Glyn had sought when there were crises in his life? Like the time after he'd fallen from the rocks near Ty Crwn (playing best-for-dying a bit too earnestly), his fractured leg held stiff in plaster of Paris for two months. He'd stayed the whole time with her, and when he'd got bored with jigsaws and reading, she'd taught him to knit after he'd become fascinated by the cables and diamonds that hung from her needles. And it was to her he'd come, straight from the train – in the first weeks after he'd gone to the secondary school in Harlech – all bloodied and crying after the Penrhyn boys had taunted and punched him because he was a sissy.

Mrs Amelia Roberts' day dreams were disturbed when a fat, red-faced woman with a cod's mouth and eyes more bloodshot than a bull dog's, squeezed onto the train in Caersws and sat opposite her across the narrow table. She smelled the rich mixture of the hill farm this country woman had left earlier somewhere deep in the folds of the hills, and Amelia Roberts remembered the goats she and Nellie Bet had herded when they were land girls. How they had both hated those goats for the way their smell clung. The cod-mouthed woman rummaged in a shopping bag and pulled out her knitting. Amelia Roberts watched the stout, fleshy fingers loop the five strands of coloured yarn dextrously around the needles in a complex sequence and she envied the woman's skill; Fair Isle had always defeated her. At Newtown the knitting was bundled back into the shopping bag. As Amelia Roberts watched the goat woman's abundant buttocks swagger along the platform into the obscurity of the station's gloom, she dabbed some *Je Reviens* onto her lace handkerchief and patted it around her neck; the perfume masked the smell and awakened some sweeter memories.

The two boys who got on the train with their mother in Welshpool needed a good hiding for the way they answered back the plain, tired-looking woman. Mrs Amelia Roberts had never heard such cheek, not even from the rough fairground crowd who descended on a winter-weary Barmouth in the days before Easter, livening the place up until their departure just before the October gales. The more brazen of the two boys reminded her of Glyn at twelve or thirteen.... Not that Glyn had ever been impudent; it was something in the boy's face, a winsome questioning look every now and then. It was just the way Glyn had looked when he'd asked her about wet dreams. That was one of the few times she'd thought to herself, "He ought to be talking to his father," but then, what a good-for-nothing Idris *Greenbank Cottage* had turned out to be. She'd never understood how Nellie Bet had put up with his womanising all those years. Of course, she knew what wet dreams were. Hadn't she slept in the same bed as her three older brothers until, one at a time, they'd left home as young men to take up their apprenticeships? But knowing didn't give her the words to speak about such things, and even as the sexual revolution went on all around them and the hippies who lived down by the quay were the talk of the town for their orgies on Ynys y Brawd, she thought it more proper to buy the boy a book by mail order from one of the Sunday newspapers. And so she helped Glyn on his way to adulthood with the gift of *Approaching Manhood* and its chapters on self-respect, honouring girls, self-restraint, and the evils of self-abuse. Glyn never asked her about sex and such things again. At the time she remembered thinking that the book must have satisfied his thirst for knowledge. But the letter he sent her from Aberystwyth some years later, just after he'd gone there to study, had set her thinking about just how badly she must have let him down.

Mrs Amelia Roberts took a taxi from the station because the hill up to the shops looked much longer and steeper than she remembered. After a freshly-cut sandwich and a cup of tea in Sidoli's (and a visit to their conveniences, which were absolutely spotless) she made straight for the Jaeger shop. She'd neither the patience, nor sadly the spirit to walk through Gullet Passage and Grope Lane, or the other eccentrically named streets and alleys that had once fascinated and invited her curiosity about the first Elizabeth's times. The assistant, who wore too much make-up, had been perhaps a little too obsequious with her *madam this* and her *madam that*. But she'd been helpful, and Amelia Roberts had left the shop in the knowledge that the suit - a cashmere and wool mix in mulberry, shot with a magenta silk thread that married the blouse - would be delivered after a minor alteration to the jacket, together with a lavishly elegant hat in navy, with gloves to match. Her shopping all done she felt suddenly weary, and walking to the taxi rank she consciously banished the voice that questioned her extravagance.... Her Glyn deserved the best. Back home and walking to Prince of Wales Crescent with the gay music of the fair ground rides cheering even the gloomiest alleys on all sides, Mrs Amelia Roberts, though quite exhausted by her excursion, brimmed with excitement and confidence, for now she knew she wouldn't let the boys down.

Sitting in the bay window of her front sitting-room with a cup of tea and a slice of the Madeira cake she'd bought at the Cancer Research sale-of-work, Amelia Roberts wondered what she might say during the service. Robert, who'd taken to calling her Anti Mill after she'd sent him letters and cards during those awful months he was in the hospital, had impressed upon her how much it would mean to them both, and naturally she couldn't refuse him. Of course she understood Robert's mother's discomfort too. Hadn't she tried for years to open Nellie Bet's mind, when she wouldn't even let Robert over the doorstep? Amelia Roberts knew that for as long as people were shunned because they were different, their public acts became acts of defiance, and so what Robert and Glyn were doing was political. She relished the role they'd asked her to play.

After the service, it wasn't Robert that people had talked about for months after, though he'd been movingly presented in his wheelchair by his mother. Nor was it the Minister, Celia, a middle-aged mother of four who'd blessed the men with unpretentious reverence. It was of Amelia Roberts that people spoke, the elegant old aunt, whose words of congratulation and encouragement for their life together, had been as vivid and precious as the magenta silk thread in her mulberry suit.

Etienne's Vineyard

They sat in the garden, an almost empty bottle of red wine on the lawn between their chairs; it was warm now from the afternoon sun, and neither of them wanted the dregs from the bottle. Lowri wondered about fetching the bottle of white from the fridge, but thought better of it once she'd realised the depths to which Hywel had sunk. When she'd suggested that they drank a glass of wine in the garden she'd thought that the six weeks of school holidays he'd spent in France had done him some good, but now she wasn't so sure.

"This Etienne, then," she said in her usual mixture of Welsh and English, "he sounds like a real *cachgi* – an absolute shit."

"No," Hywel said, shaking his head. "No, he's not; he's...." He searched the afternoon heat for some words to describe his French lover.

"He was drop-dead-gorgeous I suppose," Lowri said, "with blonde hair and a sun tan? And a big cock? Good in bed, was he?"

Hywel wiped the tears from his eyes and asked, "What

about Marc then? Has he been in touch?"

"Marc?" Lowri's face gave away the bad taste which his name left in her mouth. "Not a dickie bird, but that suits me. I don't care if I ever see him again."

"I still love him, Lowri."

"Oh! Come on, Hywel. We went through all this after he left. He's not worth it."

"I know it.... And I thought he'd stopped haunting me. It was so good to be in France, away from everything that reminded me of him, and after meeting Etienne, and letting myself fall in love again, I thought I was over him. But when I drove back from the airport yesterday, the closer I came to home, the more vividly he came back to me. You just can't stop loving someone because they decided to walk out."

"No.... I suppose that's right, but then, you didn't have to deal with all the deception."

"Last night, when I was putting the suitcases back in the box-room, I found some of his stuff in a carrier bag; some CDs, a couple of tee shirts, a pair of swimming trunks. I wore one of the tee shirts all evening and listened to his music...."

"So what about this Etienne," she interrupted, "how did you leave things with him?"

"He's coming in ten days."

"Here? To Llan-Aber?"

"I told him that if things worked out for us I'd move to Lyons."

"But Hywel *bach*, what about your job and the house?

What about all those kids who idolise you and end up more fluent in French than in English just because they want to please you. And all the work you've done on the eisteddfod committee, you can't just drop it all."

She stopped herself saying "What about me?" but she knew Hywel had heard that too.

"It seemed like a good idea at the time. Etienne asked me if I'd like to live with him and because I thought I'd got Marc out of my system I said that I'd give it some serious thought."

"But you can't just drop everything here and go'n live in France with some Frenchman you've only known for five minutes," she said, gripping his arm.

"Until Marc started to haunt me again I didn't think there was much left for me here, but now I'm confused. If I thought for a moment that he'd come back, I'd write to Etienne and tell him not to come."

Lowri thought again about the chance meeting with Marc's brother at the theatre in Harlech the week before and she changed her mind about not telling Hywel.

"There's been some talk in the village that he's in Bangor. You could call round at his mother's; she might be able to tell you something, an address or a phone number maybe."

They sat across the table from one another, their half eaten steaks, pushed around the plates and played with, not enjoyed, as good food should be. Marc drew heavily on his cigarette,

"So, go to France then, if that's what you want."

Hywel wondered what Marc would need to do to make him hate him enough to feel that he could leave. He looked into those eyes which had so often teased and invited, saying, "But I still love you, so I'm not free to go." Marc stubbed out his cigarette with such brutality that his glass of wine spilled, bleeding into the tablecloth. He swore loudly, drawing the unwanted attention of others. The waiter fussed, and as he cleared away some of the clutter that was between them he suggested that if they had finished their meal they might like to move into the bar. Marc, believing that the waiter wanted them out, felt his anger rising, "Just bring us the bill and we'll go!"

Hywel, pouring salt on to the wine stain, said, "Lowri really hates you; that's why she's been able to pick herself up and move on. It's not like that for me. I came home one day and you'd gone, and I still don't know why. You still haven't told me why."

Marc lit another cigarette, "She hates me because I started fucking her little brother; it's a good enough reason and the divorce court thought so too."

"Is that all I was for you, Marc; just someone to fuck? And all that time I thought you loved me."

"Love? Oh Hywel, you're such a bloody romantic; you've had your head too long in those French novels. Do you know what? I don't think I know what love is." Then he smiled, and through a puff of smoke he said, "But I know what good sex is. I know what I like and with you it just stopped being fun."

"For God's sake, Marc, stop it," Hywel said, shaking his

head. "You're not that empty. We had nearly three years and I know that it wasn't just about sex."

Marc leaned across the table, stabbing at the space between them with the cigarette, "You lived in your own fantasy, Hywel. You only ever saw what you wanted to see. Do you want me to tell you how many men I had during those three years? Shall I tell you?"

"You're going to tell me whether I want you to or not, Marc, so just say it."

And in the moments that they waited for the waiter to return with the bill Hywel listened and felt a knot tighten and strangle him inside. Driving back to Llan-Aber, he wondered if the scream inside him was the same as the one that had freed his sister.

Lowri passed him the salad and asked, "How did you meet him then?" Hywel's face softened as he remembered.... He was one of Cécile's friends, someone she worked with at the hospital. He'd come round for dinner on the second night after Hywel had arrived in Lyons; Cécile had thought Etienne might take him to the bars and introduce him to a few people. After dinner they'd walked from Cécile's flat near Place Sathonay, crossed the Saône by the Passerelle Saint-Georges, and wandered through the narrow streets of the old city. They'd sat in a café on the Rue Juiverie, smoked Camels and drunk a bottle of wine from Condrieu; Etienne explained that he had a house there, in his grandfather's vineyard on the slopes of the Rhône.

"I don't understand how an Englishman speaks such

good French," Etienne had said, laughing.

"But I'm not English," Hywel corrected, with a trace of irritation. "I'm from Wales; I speak Welsh with all my friends, and my French is good because I teach it in a Welsh language secondary school."

"I don't know much about the languages in England," Etienne ventured. "This Welsh, it's a dialect, is it?"

"No...." Hywel tried to remain civil. "Welsh is a Celtic language. It's much older than English."

"But you do speak English?"

"Not very often, if I can help it," Hywel answered, and tried to explain something of the sometimes bitter relationship between the Welsh and the English. As they walked back to Cécile's, Etienne asked Hywel if they could meet for dinner the next evening, just the two of them.

Hywel helped Lowri wash up the dinner dishes.

"What did you say he was, a psychiatrist?" she asked, rinsing the glasses.

"Yes," he answered. "He works some of the week in a hospital and he teaches at the medical school."

"Older than you then, is he?"

"Only a year or two."

"He's not married, is he?"

"No, Lowri. He's not married."

"So why does he want you to live together?"

"It's not just what he wants; I want it too."

"So you are lovers then," she said, tentatively.

Hywel remembered their lovemaking; their last time together, hurried, even frenzied, in the hallway of Etienne's apartment, already late, before they left for the airport. And the first time, at the house in the vineyard, gentle and nervous, taking time to discover and learn what pleased. And all those humid nights in Lyons. He smiled at his sister, "Yes, we are... and it's wonderful."

She cried and he couldn't console her.

Etienne found it strange to speak in English with Hywel but Lowri had no French so it was all they had to fall back on when the three of them were together. She'd talked about her painting; how reluctant the British were to spend on an original piece of work; how it wasn't easy to make a living as an artist and how most of the tourists to the area wanted sentimental landscapes, which she reluctantly stooped to when there was nothing in the bank to pay the bills. Over dinner they had drunk two bottles of the Condrieu from grandfather Chosson's vineyard and with coffee, Lowri started drinking the Knockando malt that Hywel had brought her, duty-free. Lowri began to talk, her words loose with alcohol.

"After my divorce I don't know what I'd have done if Hywel hadn't helped out.... Money I mean. I was so down that I couldn't paint. But you're a psychiatrist, so I don't have to explain things like that to you.... How long was it, Hywel? Nearly a year? A bit longer? And with Mam and Dad dead and buried I only had Hywel to turn to." She gulped some more whisky. "God... I'm so thankful that they were both in the grave before all that happened," she spat out, venomously. "Talk of the village, we were.... Isn't that right, Hywel? And beyond too.... Talk of the bloody county, everyone knowing our business."

She emptied her glass and poured in some more whisky, "He did tell you, did he, Etienne? He did tell you that he ran off with my husband? My dear brother and my loving husband... I loved them both and they became lovers and made me a laughing stock! Still... You've paid for it, haven't you Hywel? You've paid dearly for it! And now you, Etienne Chosson," she said, shaking her head and waving the fruit knife she'd lifted from the table in his face, "you with your suave and sophisticated French ways and your vineyard.... You want to take him away from me.... No, Monsieur Chosson," she whispered, stabbing the knife into an orange in the fruit bowl, "no! Over my dead body. My sweet little Hywel hasn't finished paying yet."

They lay in one another's arms in the deep peace that came to them after making love; all Hywel could hear, aside from Etienne's breathing, was the sea folding onto the beach below the house.

"Was she serious?" Etienne asked, breaking into the rhythm of the waves.

"She was drunk, and I'm sorry she behaved so badly."

"Yes, but does she mean what she says? Is she going to make things difficult for us?"

"I don't know.... She knows that Marc had lots of men before and after they were married, but she chooses to believe that I took him away from her, and for that she has never forgiven me…. It suits her that way."

"And does she depend on you for money?"

"Not any more. She's doing all right from the gallery…. She doesn't believe that what she's turning out is fine art, but it's commercially successful."

The waves filled the silence between them and then Hywel said, "It was the drink talking…. She won't be difficult…. Let's go to sleep."

Lowri sharpened her mother's large cloth-cutting scissors and put them in the leather shoulder bag she always took with her everywhere. She knew that they would be out; Etienne had told her how much he was looking forward to their hike over Cader Idris. She let herself in and went directly to Hywel's bedroom. She'd always liked the view from there, out across Cardigan Bay to the Llyn and Ynys Enlli; she sat in the window seat, and enjoying the view, she shredded every item of Etienne's clothing. Afterwards she pulled the light, summer quilt off Hywel's bed, and seeing the stains of their lovemaking, she plunged the scissors, through the sheet and deep into the mattress, twice, three times… Four… Again and again until she was exhausted. Then she went home and started to prepare the late supper she'd promised the two boys after their day's hike.

They sat next to one another in the window seat.

"She needs help, Hywel," Etienne said, hardly able to take it in. "Someone who can do something like this needs help and they need it soon."

"I don't know what got into her. I'm so sorry... look.... Of course, I'll pay for new clothes."

"Damn the clothes, Hywel, they're not important. She's sick. We need to see that she's cared for."

"No... she's not sick. She's just making me pay. She's trying to turn you against me and send you back to France on your own. In her mind, she's just making things even between her and me."

"Hywel, believe me, that's sick! What do you think she'll do if I don't go? Is she going to come and shred me, like she shredded my clothes?"

"That's ridiculous, Etienne. She wouldn't hurt anybody."

"Don't be so sure, my love. Remember that I work with people who do things like this."

It seemed as though there was blood everywhere. The trail went from the kitchen to the hall and on up the stairs. The mirrors in the bathroom dripped blood and his mother's old cloth-cutting scissors lay in the washbasin stained red. Hywel felt the vomit rising and heaved into the toilet bowl.

"She's in the bedroom," Etienne said. "You'd better not go in there."

"She's dead, then?" Hywel asked, kneeling in his sister's blood.

"Yes.... Perhaps she thought we'd come back last night, after we'd found my clothes. Maybe that was her intention; that we find her and get her to a hospital."

"Or maybe this was her last instalment on my debt for stealing Marc from her."

Later in the day, the police officer handed Hywel the note that Lowri had left, neatly folded in an envelope bearing his name. He read the few words she'd written in her small, neat handwriting: *"My mother's sons were angry with me, they made me keeper of the vineyards; but, my own vineyard I have not kept...." Take care of Etienne's vineyard!*

Pocket Sprung and Nested

"What about this one then?" Tom asked, the impatience of his tone cutting between them across the cluttered, Saturday morning breakfast table. Realising reluctantly that Tom wasn't going to let it drop this time, Dafydd put down the already dishevelled Travel section, poured himself another cup of coffee, and forced a smile that puffed out his ruddy cheeks above an already greying beard.

"All right," he said, without much enthusiasm, "you've got ten minutes to convince me."

Tom smiled, knowing he'd won the initial assault, but not yet sure he'd win the battle,

"This one's ideal; it's got cashmere and lambswool in the top layer, a woven damask cover, and over fifteen hundred springs nested in individual calico pockets." It was a month since Dafydd had said he thought their bed wasn't as comfortable as it used to be, and Tom's concern for him was evident in the brochures that littered the table.

"And what does all that sales-speak mean?" Dafydd

asked with grudging attention, his thoughts still immersed in the once opulent spa resorts of Central Europe.

"Well, it says here, 'the purest cashmere from Asia.... The softest lambswool from New Zealand.... These natural upholstery materials, which include cotton felt from America's Deep South and horsehair from Europe, are healthier and safer to sleep on. They won't sag....' Now, isn't that exactly what we want? You did say that your side of the bed was sagging, didn't you?"

Dafydd nodded his agreement and unconsciously rubbed the dull ache in the bottom of his back. Tom continued to read from the glossy sales catalogue.

"'They won't sag or go lumpy, and they absorb and release body moisture efficiently.'"

"That's just disgusting at breakfast time, Tom," Dafydd said, pulling a face. "I don't want to think about the mattress we sleep on absorbing all that sweat and.... Anyway, I thought that's what mattress covers are for."

Putting the brochure down and buttering the last crust-free triangle from the toast-rack, Tom's little finger made rapid, comically graceful circles in the air each time he drew the knife across the toast.

"If you ever bothered to strip our bed, my dear," he chided, "you'd appreciate why some people put their boxer shorts back on after sex."

"That's enough!" Dafydd protested. And with the slow dawning of acute embarrassment's possibility, he asked sheepishly, "Does Mrs Mac ever do the bed for us?"

"As if!" Tom said, raising both hands to his cheeks in feigned astonishment. "She doesn't even clean the toilet for us, Dafydd.... She's strictly hoovering and dusting so I don't think she'll ever blackmail you. Anyway, every man who screws, sweats and pisses gets stains on the mattress; life's like that, and who'd want any other kind of man, hmm?"

Dafydd shrugged and grimaced, "You're probably right, but I can't be doing with this kind of talk at the breakfast table. Why don't you just mark the ones in the brochures you think will do for us and I'll have a look later."

After reluctantly scanning the leaflets and accepting Tom's bribe of lunch in Chester, Dafydd conceded defeat. They were whizzing along the A55 even before the breakfast dishes had been rinsed off and stacked in the washer.

Once they'd declared their interest in the lower end of the up-market ranges the assistant at *Asleep-eezy* followed them around like a sissy's poodle.

"We'd like to take a look on our own if that's all right," Tom said, echoing her tone of forced politeness. "We'll come to you if we've got any questions."

"Oh... It's no trouble, gentlemen. I'm Mrs Chessington, the senior floor manager," she said obsequiously. "I'm here to make sure that you know exactly what kind of bed it is you want, and more importantly, to help you know what you're getting for your money once you've decided. Good beds don't come cheap, gentlemen. Now then," she said, upping her tone into the bossy range, "it's a single you're looking for, is it?"

Dafydd searched her powdered face for any hint of malevolence, while Tom countered, "Actually, no." And then, with the flair of an opera diva in his movements and defiance in his eyes, he put his arm around Dafydd and said, "We hadn't thought of moving into single beds just yet, had we darling? We're looking for a five-foot, and it has to be six-foot-six long. I mean - just look at the two of us; a bit tubby for a four-foot-six, don't you think? And it has to be firm," he said, nuzzling up to Dafydd, "We both like it firm, don't we, dear?"

"The kings are over on the far wall," Mrs Chessington sallied forth, gesturing, this time like an airhostess pointing out the emergency exits. "You might want to think about pocket springs then," she continued, beckoning them to follow her, "two ample gentlemen like yourselves." She paused, smiled a syrupy smile, and coughed, "Well, you'll need a mattress that will give each of you independent support wherever you need it. Pocket sprung mattresses take up the profile of your body and every time you change your position the mattress will cleverly adjust with you. Do come this way."

Tom knew that Dafydd wanted to leave the store; he knew, too, that they probably wouldn't buy a bed there, but once he'd started playing with Mrs Chessington the sport was just too much fun to blow the whistle on. Tom put his arm through Dafydd's and ignoring his resistance, pulled him after the saleswoman towards the king-size beds. Dafydd's discomfort grew when he noticed other customers trying too hard not to stare. Mrs Chessington, redoubtable in her olive green two-piece, described how honey-comb nested pocket springs made for a bed that was individually responsive, and how the shock waves generated as one person moved were not transmitted through the bed to disturb their sleeping partner. And like a game-show hostess announcing the star prize, she began the final movement of her sales overture.

"This one is a beautiful example of all the features I've mentioned and the English craftsmanship is outstanding." She ran her fingers along the mattress and with exaggerated reassurance she said, "It's a good eight inches deep, with these three rows of hand stitching to secure the outer springs to the border so it stays firm to the very edge. The five foot in this range has 2,346 springs, and the more springs you have, the greater the support and comfort." Patting the damask covering with its floral motifs, encouraging each of them to feel its luxuriousness, she continued, "It's an absolutely gorgeous mattress, gentlemen, upholstered with the finest quality cotton felt and 4.6 ounces of hand-teased, long-stranded, black horse hair, blended with 3 ounces of the purest lambswool to every square foot." Tom nodded his faked mindfulness while Mrs Chessington instructed, "Now, of course gentlemen, the only way you can know if a bed is right for you, is to lie on it. That's why we put these transparent plastic sheets over the bottom half of the mattresses." And shifting again into airhostess drill she gestured them both to lay beside one another with, "This particular manufacturer recommends that you take up your usual sleeping position for between ten and fifteen minutes." And after the briefest of pauses, in which even Tom was lost for words, she said, "Think about it, gentlemen. I'll give you a minute or two and I'll see if Mr Morgan is free to assist you further."

"Come on, let's cuddle up," Tom said with a smile after she'd left.

"God, don't you think I'm embarrassed enough? You've already drawn more than enough attention to us for one afternoon...."

"Oh, come on Daf. Just keep thinking about your bad back. Just another half an hour, sir, and you'll be the proud owner of a bed that will give you ten years of comfortable, health promoting, restorative, restful sleep."

"What *did* the two of you say to Mrs Chessington?" A voice rang out musically and they turned to face a ginger haired boy, his freckled face broken into a smile, his even teeth all the more white against the charcoal of his suit. Striking the campest of poses with his arms folded across his chest he continued, "She's come over all queer and had to have a sit down. Mind you," he said with a classic limp wristed gesture, "I did say to her, when we saw you coming in, that she ought to let me see to you; but there we are, that's what seniority and commission does, and the most inappropriate person dives in and ends up upsetting the customers. I'm so sorry if she embarrassed you both." He thrust his clammy hand out to be shaken with, "I'm Geoffrey Morgan, but you can call me Geoff."

"I think it's probably for us to do the apologising," Dafydd protested. "Tom did go a bit over the top with her, didn't you dear?"

"Bullshit!" Tom retorted, mirroring Geoff's stance. "I only gave as good as I got! Anyway, Geoff dear," he said, shaking the boy's hand, "why don't you sell us a bed?"

Geoffrey Morgan's impersonation of an airline steward made Mrs Chessington seem like a trainee on a government scheme but it soon became apparent that her tutelage had produced something of a clone.

"This one is a beautiful example of fine English craftsmanship," he said, running his fingers along the mattress. "It's a good eight inches deep, and with these three rows of hand stitching to secure the outer springs to the border it stays firm to the very edge. Just feel how firm it is."

Now even Dafydd began to play the shopping game as both he and Tom felt the firmness of the mattress edge, nodding their agreement with Geoff's commentary.

"Now," Geoff said, arms folded across his chest again, his hips swaying slightly, "you two are going to need a five-foot, aren't you?" They both smiled. "And probably six-foot-six long?" he asked, his right elbow shifting into his left hand, his chin nestling into the palm of the right one. "Can't have your toes hanging over the edge now, can we? Let me think now…. This range… the five foot has got 2,346 springs, and the more springs you have, the greater the support and comfort." And patting the damask covering with its floral motifs, encouraging each of them to feel its luxuriousness, he offered them again the script which Mrs Chessington had already recited.

Ridiculous though the details were, Tom and Dafydd drank in his attentiveness and savoured it.

"But let me impress upon you, gentlemen," Geoff's performance had reached its climax, his eyes expressing a message wholly absent from Mrs Chessington's pitch, "the only way you can know if a bed is going to be right for you, is to lie on it."